DINO-WRESTLING

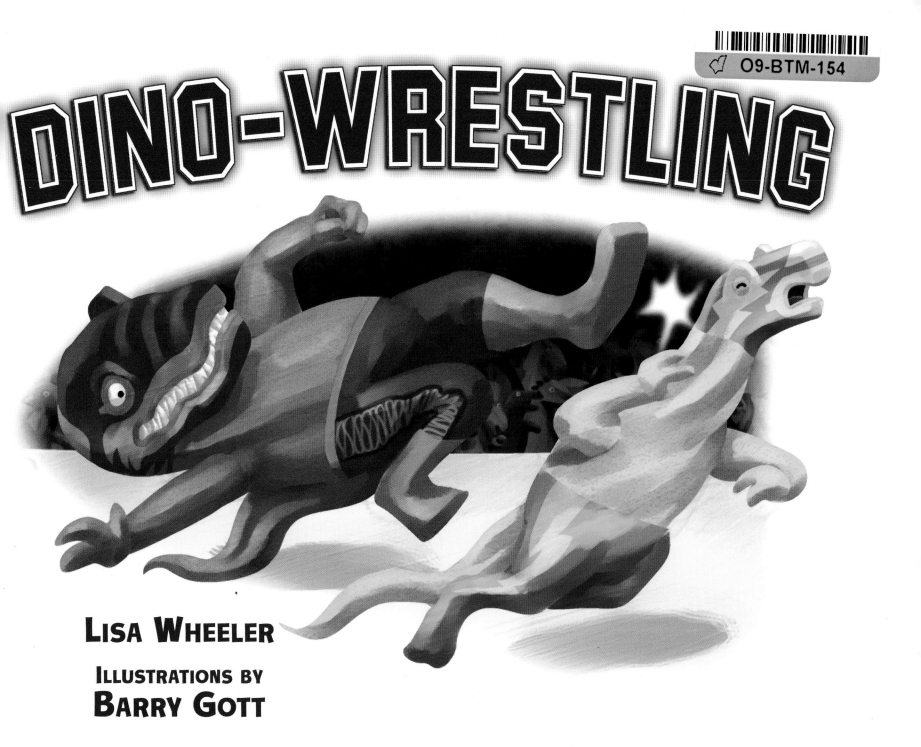

LISA WHEELER

ILLUSTRATIONS BY
BARRY GOTT

CAROLRHODA BOOKS MINNEAPOLIS

For the Grasso family—Casey, Becky, Dakotah,
and especially Hunter and Mason, who showed
me all their wrestling moves —L.W.

For Rose, Finn, and Nandi —B.G.

Text copyright © 2013 by Lisa Wheeler
Illustrations copyright © 2013 by Barry Gott

Carolrhoda Books
A division of Lerner Publishing Group, Inc.
241 First Avenue North
Minneapolis, MN 55401 USA

For reading levels and more information,
look up this title at www.lernerbooks.com.

Library of Congress Cataloging-in-Publication Data

Wheeler, Lisa, 1963-
    Dino-wrestling / by Lisa Wheeler ; illustrated by Barry Gott.
        p.   cm
    Summary: Meat-eating and vegetarian dinosaurs clash at
the wrestling jamboree, demonstrating such styles as sumo,
Greco-Roman, and lucha libre.
    ISBN 978-1-4677-0212-6 (lib. bdg. : alk. paper)
    ISBN 978-1-4677-1616-1 (eBook)
    [1. Stories in rhyme. 2. Dinosaurs—Fiction. 3. Wrestling—Fiction.]
I. Gott, Barry, illustrator. II. Title.
PZ8.3.W5668Dk 2013
[E]—dc23   2012049251

Manufactured in the United States of America
2 - CG - 12/1/13

Dinosaurs get pumped for action!
It's the weekend's main attraction.

What's the sport they came to see?
The Dino-Wrestling Jamboree!

Athletes travel many miles,
compete in different wrestling styles.

FOLKSTYLE

LUCHA

LIBRE

Step inside the massive tent.
Get ready for the first event.

GRECO-ROMAN

SUMO

FREE-STYLE

PRO TAG TEAM

ALLOSAURUS -VS- ANKYLOSAURUS

The folkstyle wrestling mat is round with painted lines to mark the bounds.

Allo and **Ankylo** take their stance within the circle. Here's their chance!

One-piece singlets: green and red.
Protective gear goes on their heads.

Both sides hope that their guy wins.
The whistle blows! The match begins.

FOLKSTYLE WRESTLING

Ankylo has amazing talents—
watch him throw Allo off-balance!

The green-clad grappler gets a grip.
Doesn't let his cradle slip.

The ref counts down and—**Boom**—it's done.
It's Ankylo's match! He's number one!

What's this?
The **Pterodactyl Twins**
are dressed in singlets,
sneaking in.

But this is not the **Twins'** event.
Security throws them out the tent!

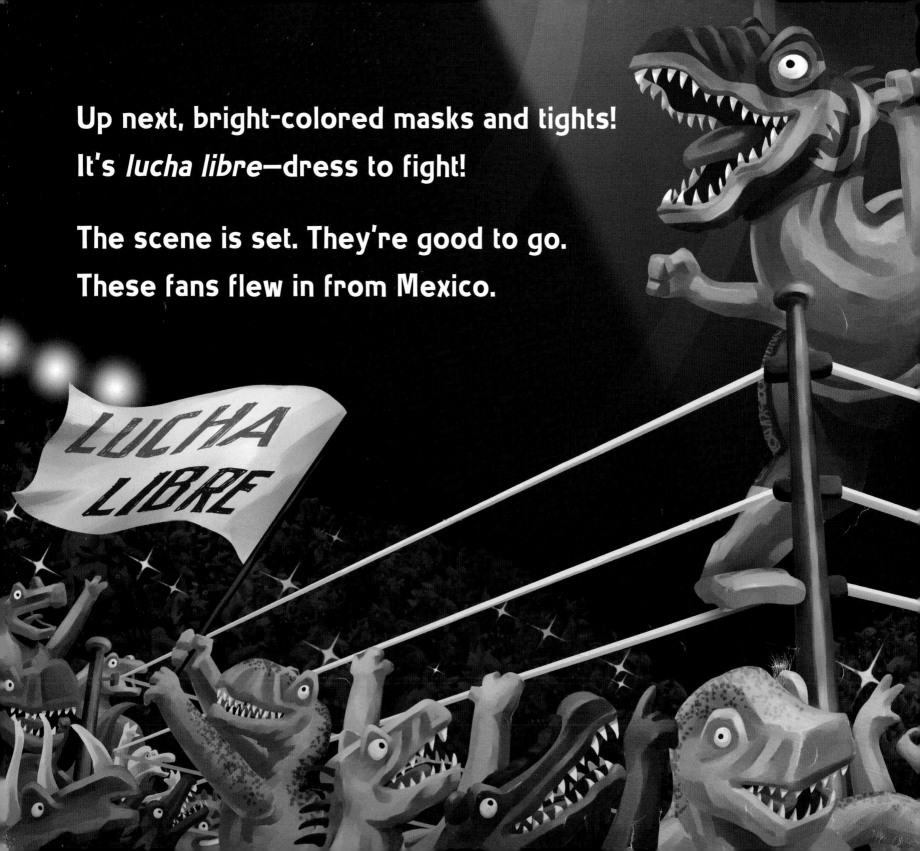

Up next, bright-colored masks and tights!
It's *lucha libre*—dress to fight!

The scene is set. They're good to go.
These fans flew in from Mexico.

Tarbosaurus as El Diablo
plays the bad boy—he's the *rudo*.

Victorious Verde—that's Iguano—
he's the good-guy *técnico*.

Flipping, flying 'round the ring.
Bounding, bouncing like a spring.

The crowd goes loco—shouts and boos.
Ouch! That hit will leave a bruise.

It's hard to tell which guy's ahead
till **Verde** gets knocked in the head.

El Diablo wins this round.

The fans protest and come unwound.

Greco-Roman style is next—
Stegosaurus and T. Rex.

Face-to-face, backs to the crowd,
the biggest rule: no legs allowed!

T. Rex's arms are way too short.
Why did he ever choose this sport?

He's on the ground in no time flat.
Stego pins him to the mat!

The second go is a repeat.
Stego wins! T. Rex is beat.

The Twins again? "No! No! No!
There's the door! Out you go!"

GIGANOTOSAURUS
-vs-
TRICERATOPS

Here is a match in the sumo tradition,
an ancient observance of Shinto religion.

They stand on the *dohyo*, each looming large,
crouch low, face-to-face, ready to charge.

Tricera moves first! Gigano is ready.
Each pushes the other. Both dinos hold steady.

Gigano is gaining. Tricera's undone.
He's forced out the ring! Gigano has won!

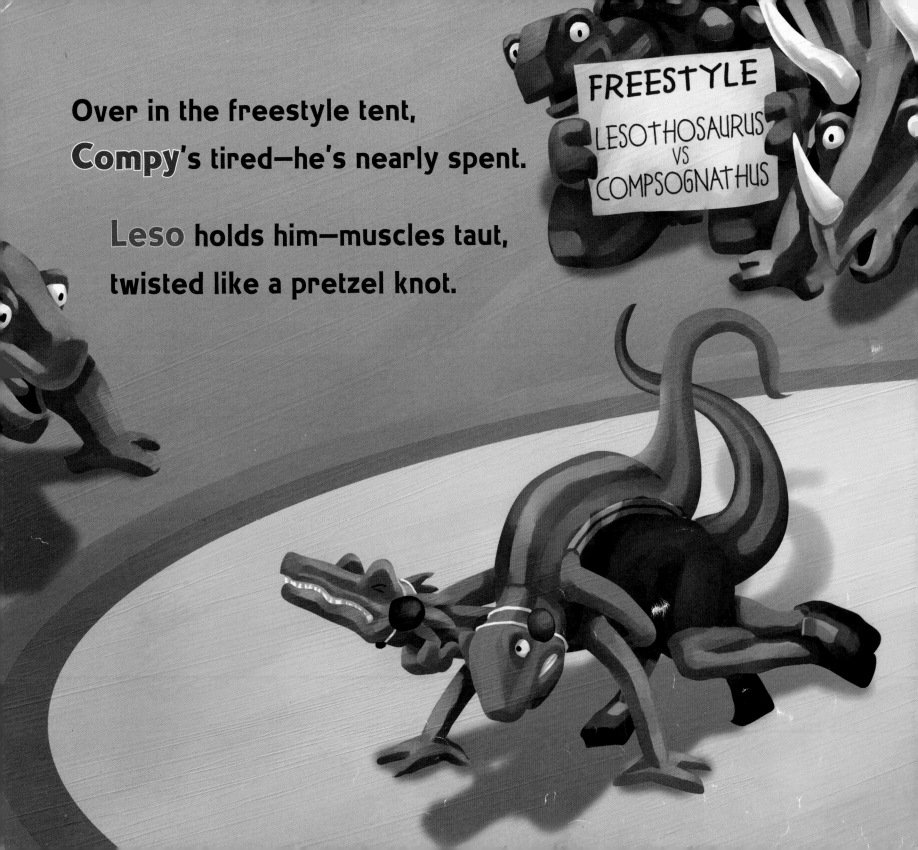

Over in the freestyle tent,
Compy's tired—he's nearly spent.

Leso holds him—muscles taut,
twisted like a pretzel knot.

FREESTYLE
LESOTHOSAURUS
VS
COMPSOGNATHUS

Each one fights to get the pin
or score some points to earn the win.

But **Leso** keeps the upper hand
till **Compy** tries another plan.

This match is **ON!** It's no rehearsal.

He turns, unties, and then . . . reversal!

Compy leans in—holds him flat.
Leso's shoulders touch the mat.

And that is that!

Not again!
Those sneaky guys
don't fool the refs with their disguise.

Many dinosaurs pay to see
the superstars of the WWD.

The showy tag teams take their places.
Aren't those two familiar faces?

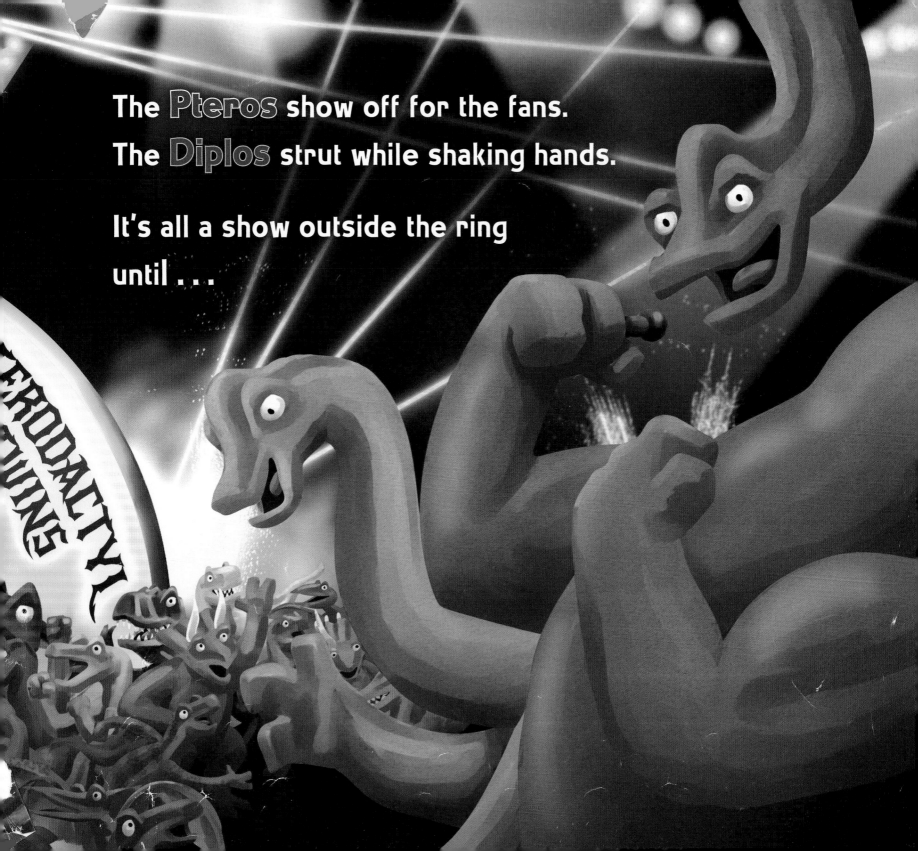

The Pteros show off for the fans.
The Diplos strut while shaking hands.

It's all a show outside the ring
until . . .

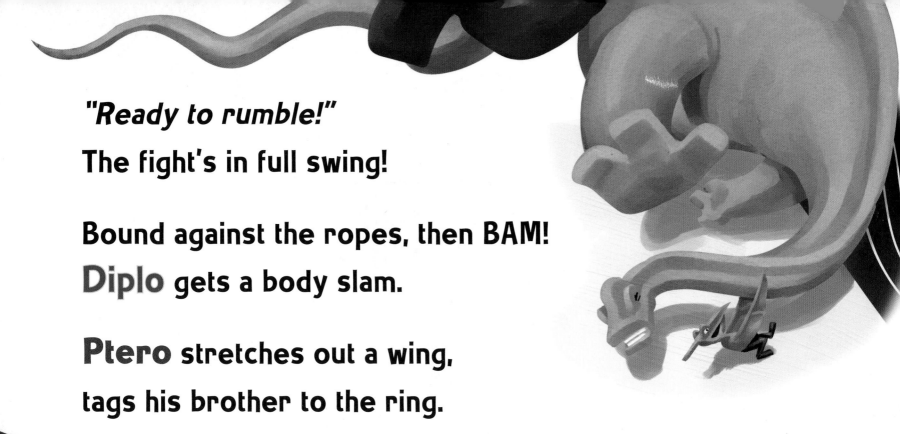

"Ready to rumble!"
The fight's in full swing!

Bound against the ropes, then BAM!
Diplo gets a body slam.

Ptero stretches out a wing,
tags his brother to the ring.

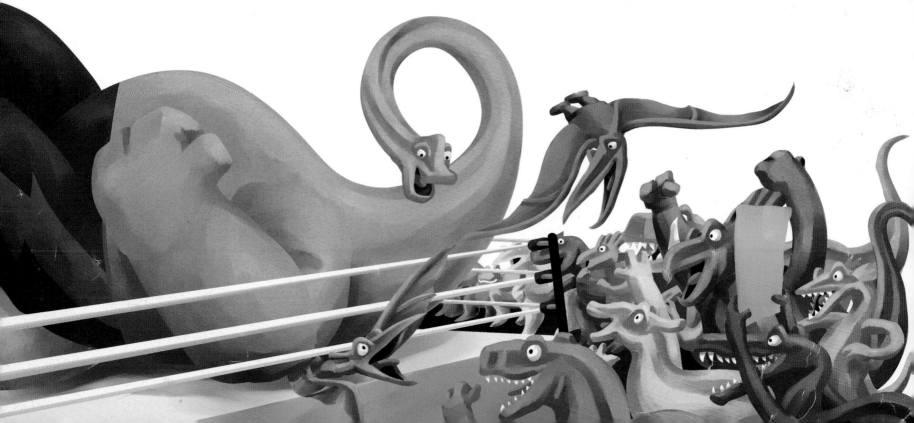

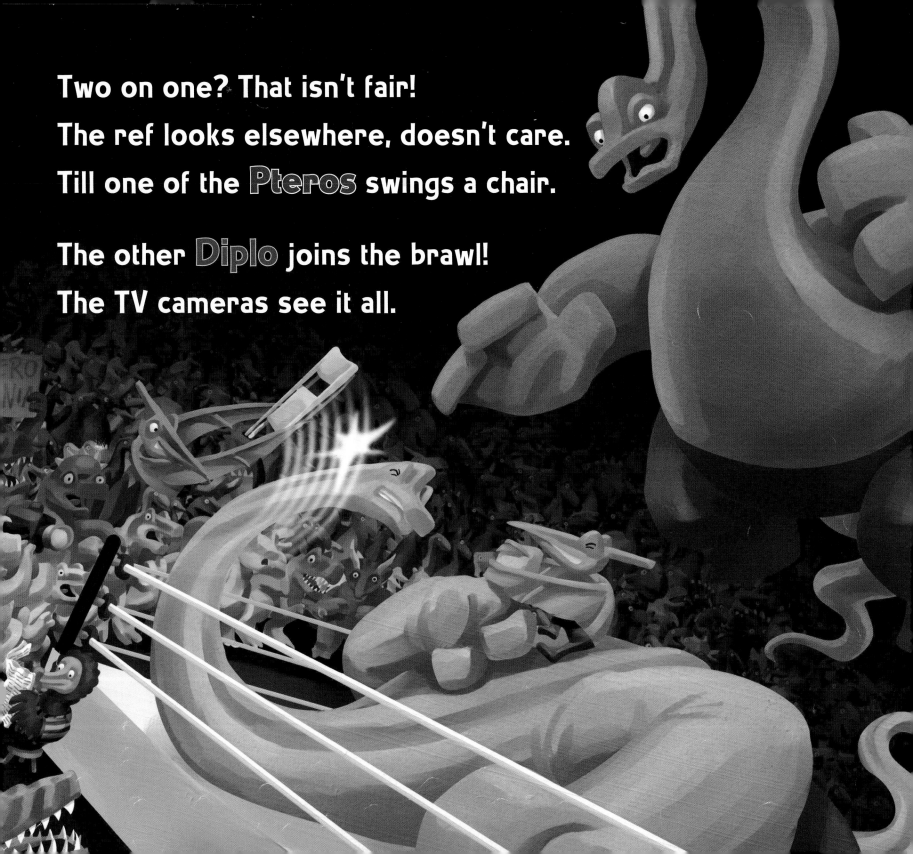

Two on one? That isn't fair!
The ref looks elsewhere, doesn't care.
Till one of the Pteros swings a chair.

The other Diplo joins the brawl!
The TV cameras see it all.

As officials call for quiet,
fans join in. Now it's a riot!

The tent falls down. There's no more fun.
The wrestling jamboree is done.

But what will fans do for the rest of the year?

Dino-boarding is totally here!